Life of a Military Child™

Danielle is Resilient

By: Patisha Johnson and CMSAF JoAnne Bass

ISBN: 978-163972682-4

Dr. Kenneth Ginsburg, M.D., M.S., Ed, established a framework and methodology guiding parents, families, and communities towards developing their children to be more resilient. He outlined how the 7C's: connection, competence, confidence, character, contribution, coping, and control are essential components of building resilience.

What's the point of our military children being resilient? Why is it important? How can we get started instilling these principles in our children?

This installment of Life of a Military Child showcases Danielle bringing the answers to these questions to life. She encounters a stressful situation and connects with her friends and family working towards a solution. She's one tough cookie! Being a military kid can be hard sometimes but you're never alone and the Life of a Military Child series will show some great ways for families to wrap their children in love and overcome the obstacles in their lives.

As a bonus, Danielle's story has a mini-scavenger hunt built-in. As you read with your child, see if they can find all the bold words that are the essential building blocks of resilience.

Hi, I'm Danielle!
These are my best friends...

Danielle was born in Mililani, Hawaii, and has lived on four military bases. Her mother works from home and takes care of her and Ozzy.

Her dad is a First Sergeant in his unit. He spends a lot of time taking care of people in need.

Danielle likes going to school because she gets to see her best friends. She also likes to help her mom around the house. Her mom lets her help load the dishwasher, and Ozzy eats the bubbles - he's funny!

Ozzy has always been in Danielle's life. They do everything together; he keeps her safe at night by sleeping on her bed.

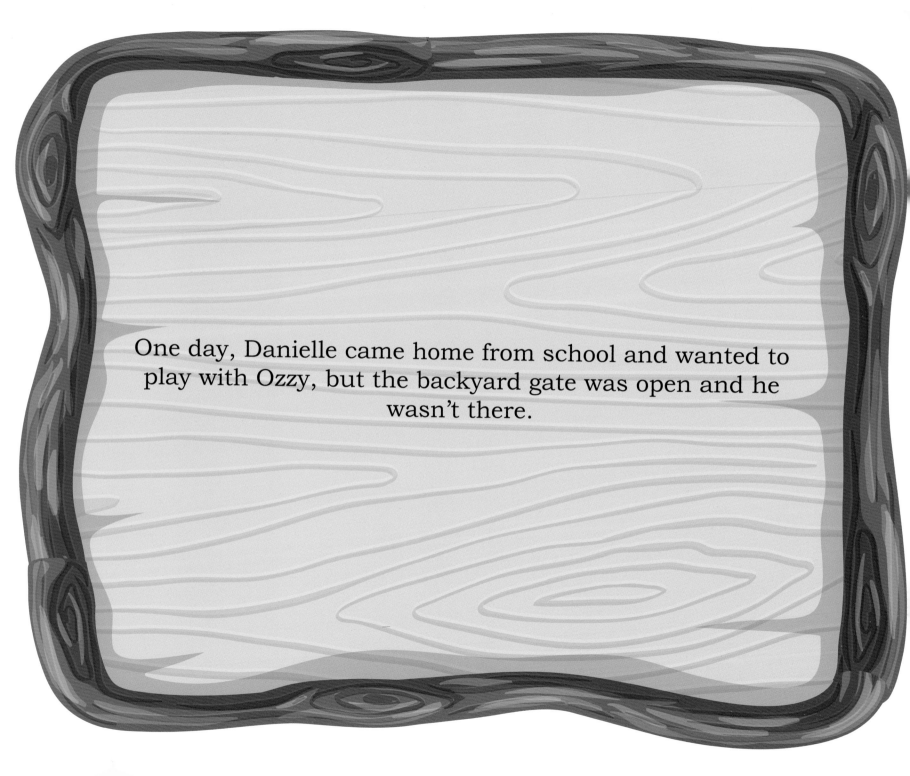

One day, Danielle came home from school and wanted to play with Ozzy, but the backyard gate was open and he wasn't there.

Ozzy and Danielle like to play games, so maybe he started playing hide-and-seek to surprise her when she came home from school.

"Ozzy...where are you? I'm coming to find you!" Danielle shouted playfully.

I'll look in the kitchen first... that's where he likes to eat his treats.
"Ozzy? Are you in here?" Danielle asked.

Danielle's mom asked, "Danielle is that you?"

"Hi, mommy. Ozzy and I are playing hide-and-seek and he's winning," Danielle said.

"Ok, sweet girl, you two have fun and I'm going to start dinner," Danielle's mom said.

I'll look in my room. Maybe he got tired and took a nap on my bed.

"Ahhh rats! He's not here either," Danielle said.

Danielle went back downstairs to check in the living room behind the couch.

"Mom, Dad! Have you seen Ozzy?" Danielle asked.

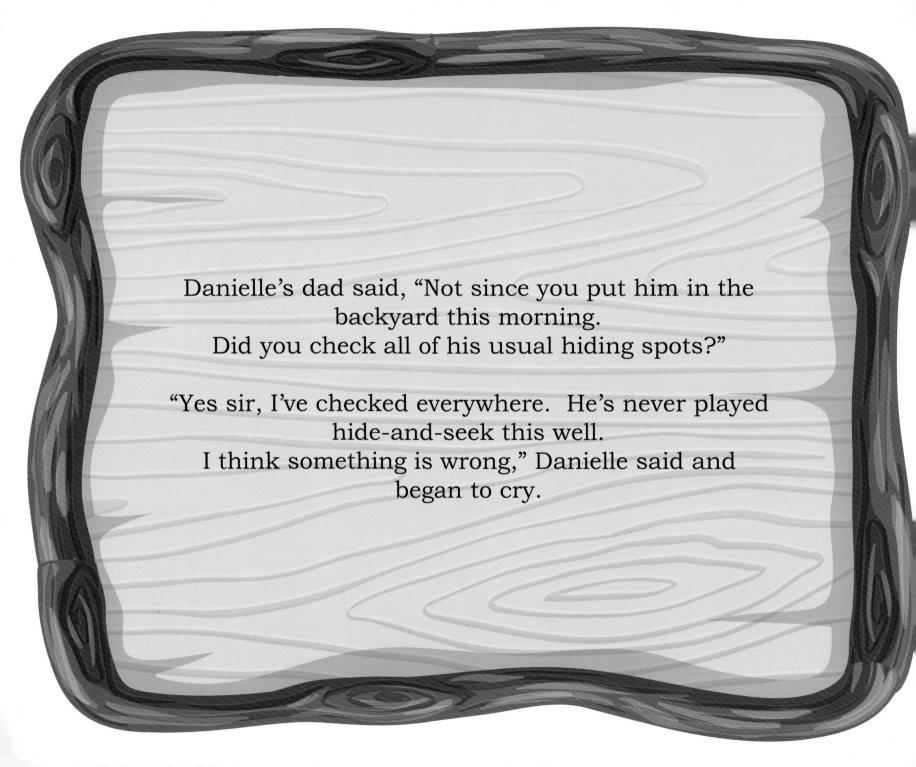

Danielle's dad said, "Not since you put him in the backyard this morning.
Did you check all of his usual hiding spots?"

"Yes sir, I've checked everywhere. He's never played hide-and-seek this well.
I think something is wrong," Danielle said and began to cry.

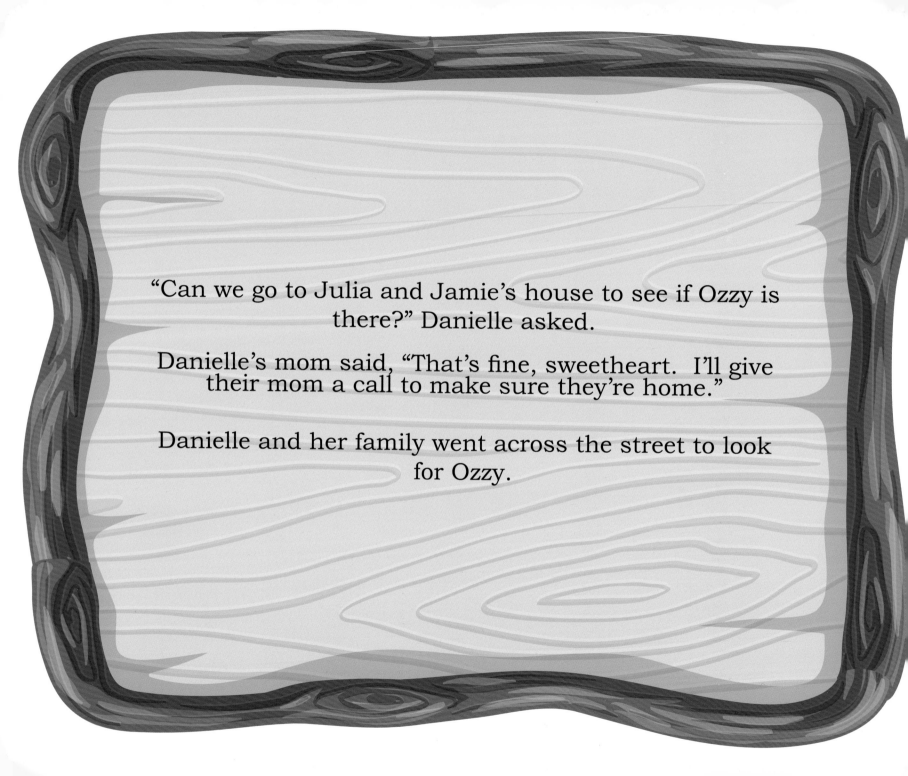

"Can we go to Julia and Jamie's house to see if Ozzy is there?" Danielle asked.

Danielle's mom said, "That's fine, sweetheart. I'll give their mom a call to make sure they're home."

Danielle and her family went across the street to look for Ozzy.

"Julia, Jamie! I can't find Ozzy. Have you seen him?" Danielle asked.

"No, we haven't seen him, but we'll help you find him," the girls replied.

A tear ran down Danielle's cheek.

Julia and Jamie's mom said, "Girls, do you remember how we learned to **control** our feelings by taking a deep breath and making a plan when we lose things?"

"Yes ma'am!" the girls shouted.

"Let's plan a search and rescue party!" Danielle said excitedly.

"It's time for OPERATION FIND OZZY!
We need a map, paper, markers, doggie treats, and
Ozzy's favorite toy." Danielle said.

"We'll be right back." Julia and Jamie said before
running upstairs.

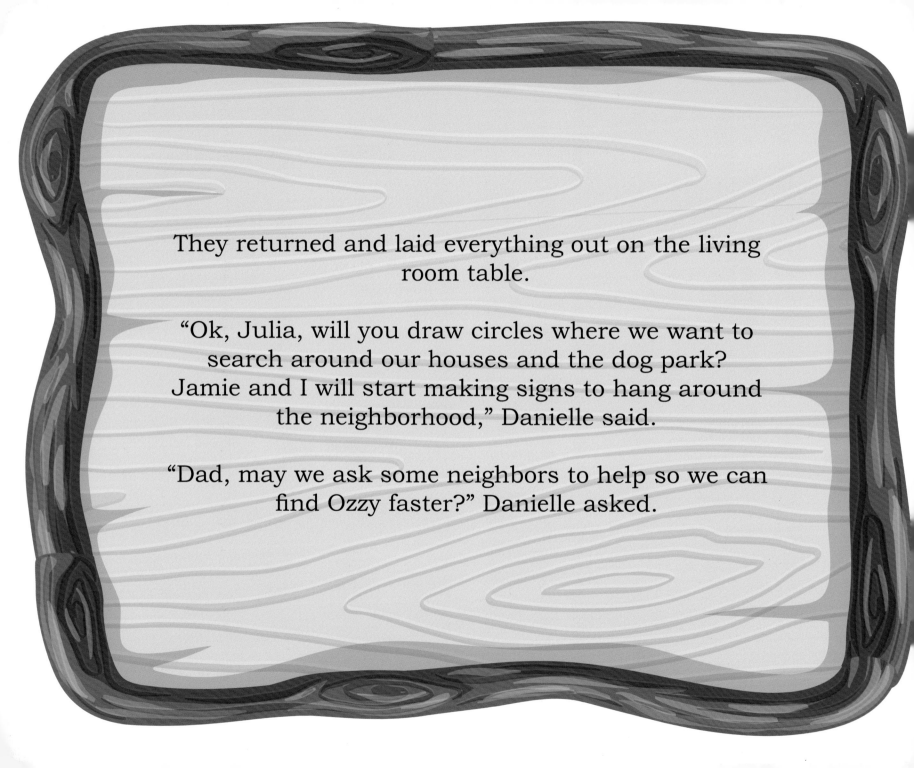

They returned and laid everything out on the living room table.

"Ok, Julia, will you draw circles where we want to search around our houses and the dog park? Jamie and I will start making signs to hang around the neighborhood," Danielle said.

"Dad, may we ask some neighbors to help so we can find Ozzy faster?" Danielle asked.

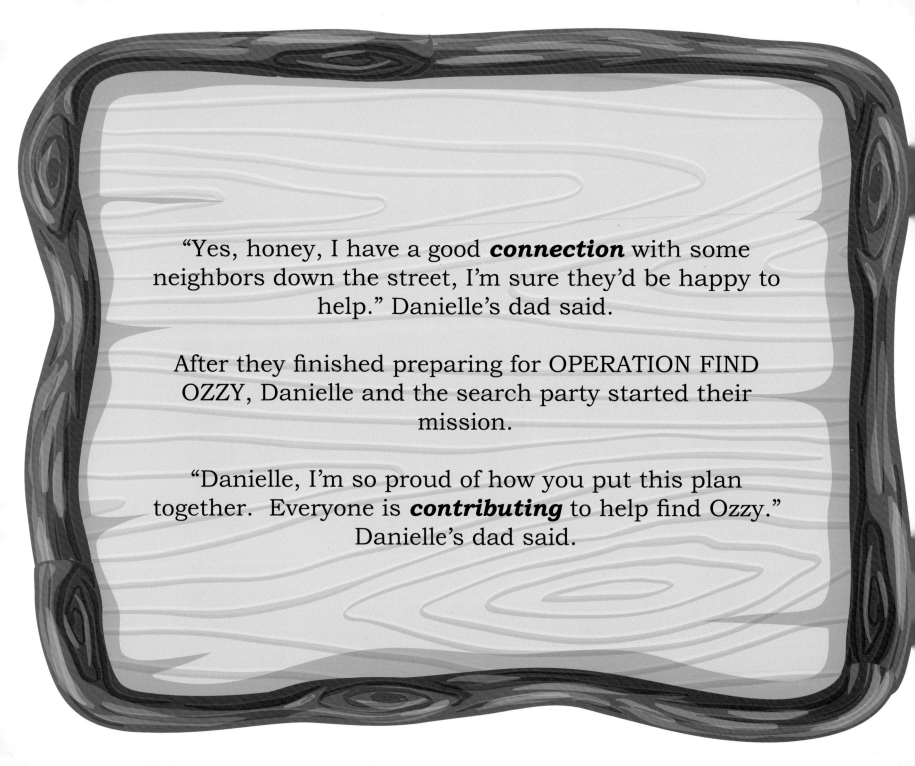

"Yes, honey, I have a good **connection** with some neighbors down the street, I'm sure they'd be happy to help." Danielle's dad said.

After they finished preparing for OPERATION FIND OZZY, Danielle and the search party started their mission.

"Danielle, I'm so proud of how you put this plan together. Everyone is **contributing** to help find Ozzy." Danielle's dad said.

As they searched around their street, some neighbors joined the search party and helped hang flyers.

One of the neighbors said, "Danielle, here are some walkie-talkies I found in our garage. We can use them to keep in touch."

Ewwww...no one uses those anymore, download this app instead," Danielle said.

Danielle's dad said, "Hey team, let's split up to cover more ground before it gets too dog-gone dark."

"Too soon, Dad!" Danielle said.

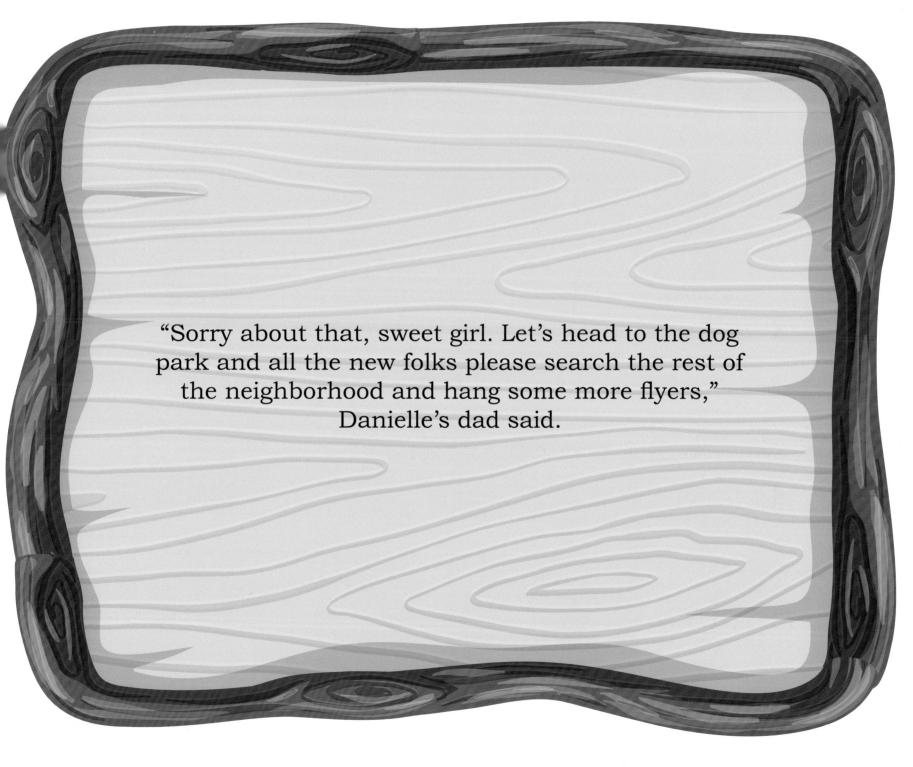

"Sorry about that, sweet girl. Let's head to the dog park and all the new folks please search the rest of the neighborhood and hang some more flyers," Danielle's dad said.

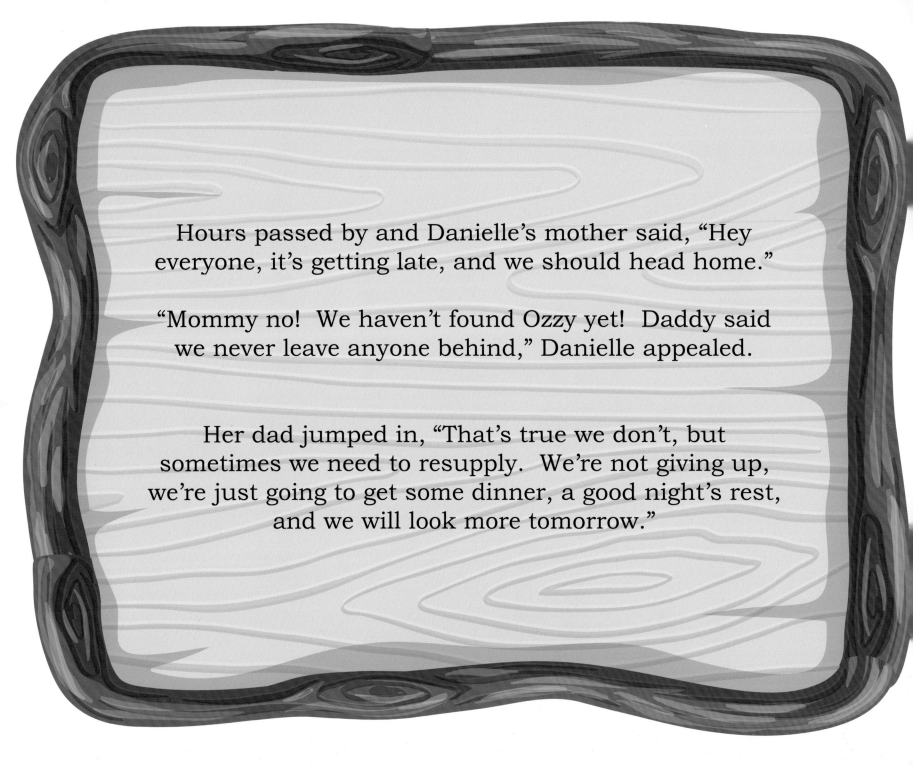

Hours passed by and Danielle's mother said, "Hey everyone, it's getting late, and we should head home."

"Mommy no! We haven't found Ozzy yet! Daddy said we never leave anyone behind," Danielle appealed.

Her dad jumped in, "That's true we don't, but sometimes we need to resupply. We're not giving up, we're just going to get some dinner, a good night's rest, and we will look more tomorrow."

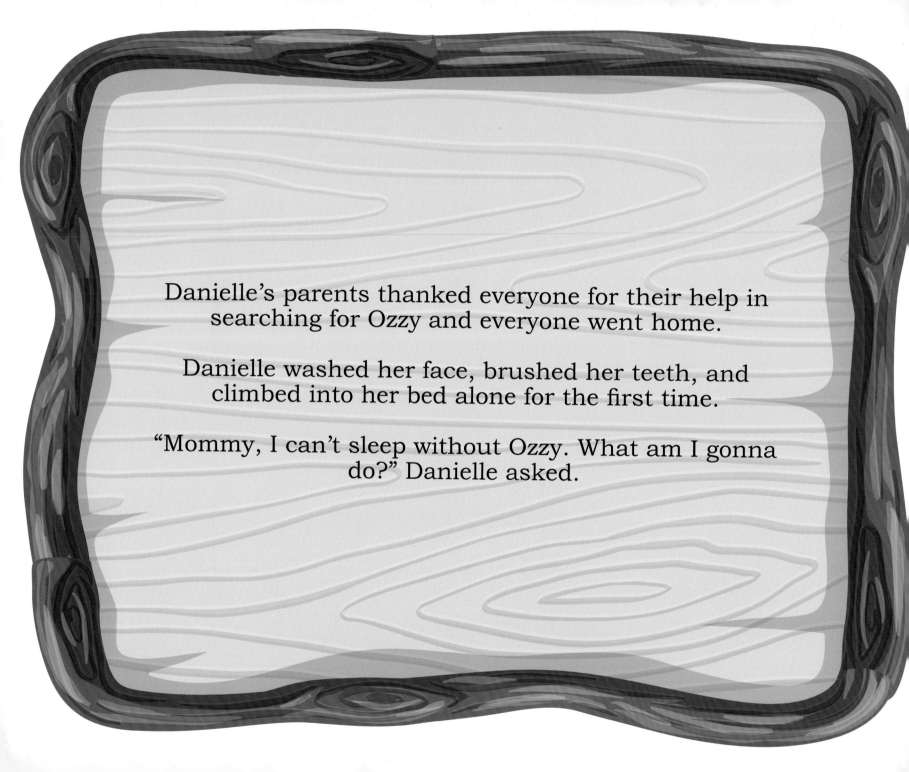

Danielle's parents thanked everyone for their help in searching for Ozzy and everyone went home.

Danielle washed her face, brushed her teeth, and climbed into her bed alone for the first time.

"Mommy, I can't sleep without Ozzy. What am I gonna do?" Danielle asked.

"We have to be brave and **confident** knowing we have good friends helping us.

"Hold on to this pillow really tight and have sweet dreams," Danielle's mom said.

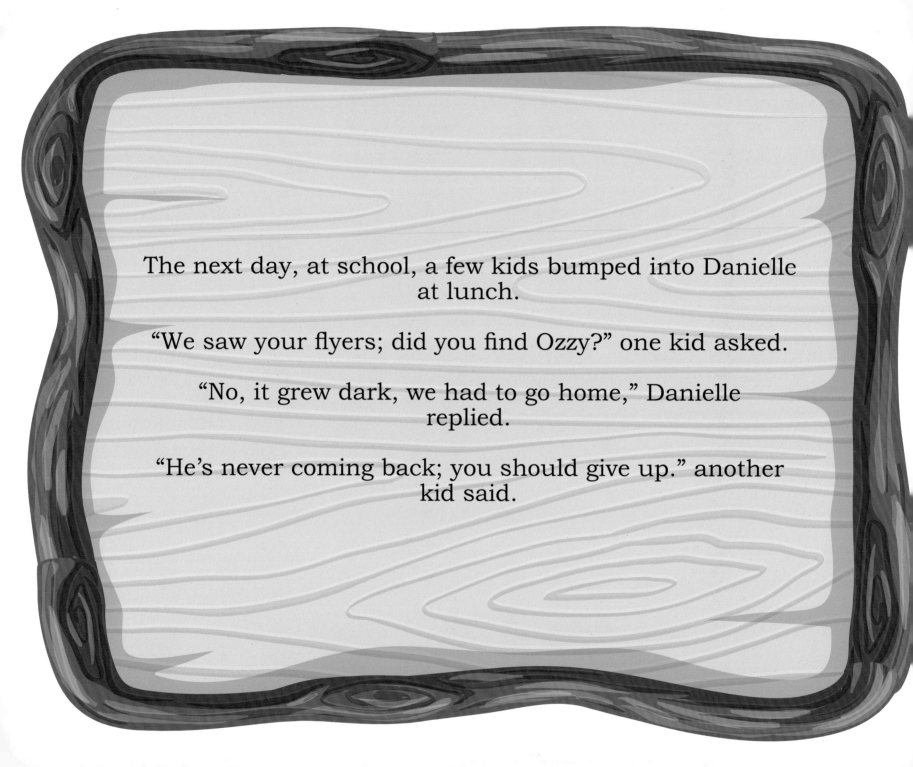

The next day, at school, a few kids bumped into Danielle at lunch.

"We saw your flyers; did you find Ozzy?" one kid asked.

"No, it grew dark, we had to go home," Danielle replied.

"He's never coming back; you should give up." another kid said.

Danielle started crying and thought to herself, maybe they're right...maybe I'll never see Ozzy again.

Julia saw Danielle crying and hugged her.

Julia said, "I have a secret. I lost my favorite necklace that my grandmother gave me. I know it feels bad to lose something very important to you. Whatever you do, don't give up on OPERATION FIND OZZY."

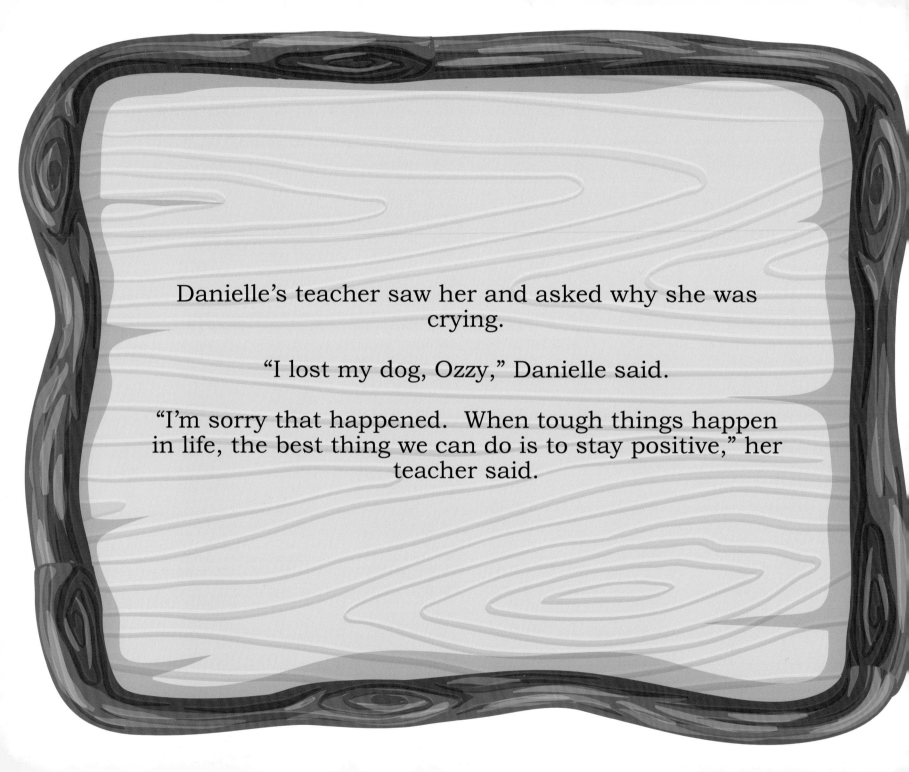

Danielle's teacher saw her and asked why she was crying.

"I lost my dog, Ozzy," Danielle said.

"I'm sorry that happened. When tough things happen in life, the best thing we can do is to stay positive," her teacher said.

"Is that why Julia hugged you?" her teacher asked.

"Yes, ma'am. She helped me look for Ozzy last night," Danielle said.

Her teacher said, "Relying on friends is a great way to **cope** as you work through hard times. That's a special **connection** you two have. It's nice to have good friends."

Danielle's mom picked her up from school.

"Is Daddy home from work yet?" Danielle asked.

"Not yet, he's out doing what First Sergeants do, taking care of people," Danielle's mom said.

"After we find Ozzy, I want to help people just like my Daddy," Danielle replied.

"Mommy, look! Someone is in our driveway; maybe they found Ozzy!" Danielle said.

"Good afternoon, ma'am. My name is First Sergeant Perry, and I work with your husband. I live a few streets down and I think I found Ozzy."

Ozzy started barking and scratching at the window in the front seat.

"That's Ozzy!" Danielle screamed.

First Sergeant Perry opened the door and Ozzy ran over and knocked Danielle down, licking her all over, and wagging his tail with excitement.

Ozzy, I'm so glad you're back! I was so worried about you.

Julia and Jamie heard the commotion and came across the street just as First Sergeant Perry was leaving.

"We did it! OPERATION FIND OZZY was a success!" all the girls screamed together as Ozzy ran circles around them, jumping up and down.

The End

Resiliency Lesson from LOAMC:

Danielle's perseverance paid off and she learned how to **connect** with others
who care when dealing with tough situations. She worked within the things she
could **control**, struggled with her emotions at times, but ultimately overcame
that fear with the support of her friends and family. Instead of withdrawing to
herself, Danielle took a different path and communicated her feelings, asked for
help, and grew stronger. Life does not always go according to plans but Danielle
helped show us some tools to use to become more resilient in the face of
adversity.

#BetterTogether

Let's review the lessons Danielle learned, so you can load up your toolbox.

It's pop quiz time!
Were you able to find all the bold words and help Danielle get Ozzy home safely? Wow, you did great – you're such a great helper! Let's talk about those "Cs" a little bit more so you can be strong like Danielle. Resilience is being able to deal with change and keep pushing forward. Think about it like you're playing games with your friends and you lose. Do you give up? Of course not! You practice, focus on your moves, and try harder next time. That's how real life is too, you keep working hard and maintain a positive attitude as you work through problems. Ask for help from your friends and family and work together as a team.

Control. With so much change around them, military children need a sense of ownership over some aspects of their lives and environment. Danielle was a real trooper when she came up with the search and rescue plan and gave tasks to her friends and family. She focused on what she could control to make an impact on her tough situation.

Connection. This is having close ties to your family, friends, and community. In this story, Danielle's connection to her best friends gave her hope and comfort when she was sad. Talking to Julia and hearing her story help to reassure her to never give up.

Contribution. Many were concerned and wanted to help find Ozzy. Danielle and her dad, was able to rally up neighbors and friends. They all brought awareness to the search by placing flyers throughout the community. This allowed many to contribute in the search for finding Ozzy.

Confident. Having a positive self-image is important as kids grow up. When Danielle's Mom told her that her Dad would be proud of her for wanting to help people that helped to grow her confidence. Recognizing our children when they do well reinforces their value system and allows them to believe in their abilities.

Coping. Managing stress, avoiding destructive thoughts, and worrisome behaviors allow our children to better address and overcome the problem sets in front of them. Danielle's teacher did a great job of talking to her encouraging her to rely on her friends. Realizing she was not alone allowed her to redirect her thoughts of giving up after being teased at school and persevere until the end.

Be sure to check out our other LOAMC book series,
where we share more lessons to help not only military children,
but ALL children, navigate life.